Jenny and the Cornstalk

Retold by Gare Thompson
Illustrated by Lane Yerkes

STECK-VAUGHN
COMPANY
ELEMENTARY • SECONDARY • ADULT • LIBRARY

Contents

Jenny Trades Her Cow

Once upon a time, there was a young girl named Jenny. She lived with her grandfather on a small farm.

Jenny and her grandfather were very poor. They worked hard, but few plants grew in their rocky land. Often all they had for food was their old cow's milk. One day the cow had no milk left.

"Grandfather!" cried Jenny. "What will we do?"

3

Grandfather said, "We'll have to sell the cow. We can use the money to buy food."

Jenny brushed the cow and tied a ribbon around her neck. Jenny took her to the market, but no one wanted to buy the old cow.

Jenny walked home sadly. She passed a man on the road. He stopped and asked her, "Why are you so sad?"

Jenny patted her cow and said, "No one will buy my cow."

"I have no money, but I'll trade these seeds for your cow," said the man.

"What kind of seeds are they?" Jenny asked.

The seeds hopped in the man's hand. "They're good luck seeds. They make wishes come true," he said.

Jenny traded her cow for the seeds. She looked down at them and made a wish never to be hungry again. When Jenny looked up, the man and the cow were gone.

Jenny ran home with the good luck seeds. She wanted to plant them right away.

"Grandfather, come see what I have!" cried Jenny. "I traded the cow for three lucky seeds."

"What do you mean?" Grandfather asked. "I've never heard of lucky seeds. They look like plain old seeds to me."

"Well, let's plant them and see," said Jenny. They planted the seeds in the garden.

9

Jenny Makes a Friend

The next morning, Jenny looked out of her window. She saw a huge, green cornstalk. The cornstalk was so tall that it touched the clouds.

Jenny called, "Grandfather, come and look! You won't believe your eyes! One of our seeds grew into a giant cornstalk. It goes way up into the clouds. I wonder what's up there. I think I'll climb to the top."

"Be careful. Just look around and come right back," Grandfather called after her. He picked up an ear of corn and smiled. Dinner!

Jenny climbed up through the clouds until she saw a huge castle. A giant woman was standing by the castle door. She was brushing flour off her hands.

"Hello, little girl. How did you get here?" asked the woman.

"I climbed to the top of this cornstalk to see what's here," said Jenny. "Wow! I've never seen a castle before. It's beautiful."

"Yes, it's a lovely castle for giants. My husband and I live here," said the woman. "We must be very quiet. He's sleeping inside, and we'd better not wake him. He's not a friendly giant."

12

14

"Oooh! What smells so good?" Jenny asked. She was hungry from her long climb.

"It's a tasty sandwich that I made from fresh bread. Would you like some?" asked the woman.

"Oh, yes, I'm very hungry," said Jenny. "It was a long climb, and I haven't had any lunch."

"Well, I'd be glad to share," said the woman in a kind voice. "If you're that hungry, please take the whole sandwich. Now you must leave quickly. I think I hear my husband coming."

The Giant Wakes Up

"FEE, FI, FO, FEED! My tasty sandwich is what I need," roared the giant. "My very own sandwich, just for me."

16

The woman said, "It's all gone. I shared it with a hungry little girl."

"What? You shared?" yelled the giant. **"FEE, FI, FO, FAIR!** I do not want to share! I'm getting my sandwich back."

The giant ran to find the girl, but she was gone. Jenny had taken the sandwich and climbed down the cornstalk.

Jenny and Grandfather ate the giant sandwich. When it was gone, Jenny climbed the cornstalk again.

Jenny saw the woman and said, "Thank you for the sandwich. I shared it with my grandfather. It was yummy."

The kind woman said, "Well, if you're hungry again, take this pizza. It's fresh from the oven, and I'd be glad to share it with you."

18

19

Suddenly, Jenny heard giant footsteps. The kind woman patted Jenny's hand and pulled her close.

"FEE, FI, FO, FEED! My tasty pizza is what I need!" roared the giant.

The kind woman said, "Wait! This little girl is hungry, and you should share. Can't you eat something else?"

"FEE, FI, FO, FAIR! I do not want to share! But...I guess I could eat my stew instead," grumbled the giant.

Jenny smiled to herself. The kind woman gave her the pizza. Jenny knew Grandfather would love it.

The New Friends Share

Later, Jenny wanted to say thank you to the kind woman, so she went to the castle again. The giant opened the door!

Jenny was very brave and said, **"FEE, FI, FO, FEED!** A little friend is what YOU need."

22

The giant's face lit up. He said, **"FEE, FI, FO, FAIR!** Even giants learn to share!"

Jenny smiled at the giant. He handed her three bean seeds and said, "They're good luck seeds. They make wishes come true."

"Oh, thank you. I'll share them with my cousin, Jack," Jenny said. She put the seeds in her pocket and waved goodbye.

23

Jenny and Grandfather lived happily
ever after. And Jenny often wondered if
Jack ever planted the three bean seeds.

24